# The Big Dance

SHIRLIE CALABRESE

The Big Dance
Copyright © 2023 Shirlie Calabrese



Because of the dynamic nature of the Internet, any web addresses or links contained in this book may have changed since publication and may no longer be valid. The views expressed in this work are solely those of the author and do not necessarily reflect the views of the publisher, and the publisher hereby disclaims any responsibility for them.

Library of Congress Control Number:    2023911872

Paperback:    979-8-9886071-3-7

Jennifer and Alex met and became friends when they were in the Madison Middle School in New Jersey. They were in seventh grade and had the same dance classes together. Mrs. Lands was their dance instructor from seventh grade all through high school. Alex was an exceptional dancer and Jennifer was his partner in many of the shows they were in during their four years of high school. They both had many dance moves they worked on to make the basic moves much different.

When they were in their senior year, Mrs. Lands felt that they would qualify to enter the East Coast Dance Contest that was being held in New York during their Senior year. She talked to them and their parents about entering the competition. Alex, Jennifer and both their parents felt this would be an awesome competition for them to be in. They made arrangements to meet with Mrs. Lands so they could fill out the all the entry forms. The competition was for seniors only, so this was an opportunity that they had to stay committed to and continue their dance classes.

Jennifer and Alex had been long awaiting and looking forward to being accepted for the East Coast Dance Contest. It seemed like such a long time since they filled out all the entry forms for the dance contest to celebrate their senior high school graduation.

Just before graduation in June, Jennifer got off the bus from school and got the mail from her mailbox. She saw a letter from "East Coast Dance Contest" in the pieces of mail. As soon as she got into the house she opened the mail from them and read all about the contest and that her and Alex were accepted to be in the contest. Jennifer read the letter again. This is wonderful, she thought. I've got to call Alex right now. As she waited for him to answer the phone, she could feel her heart pounding. "Hello, Alex. Guess what came in the mail today!" Alex wasn't in the mood for guessing games; his day had started out bad when he was late for school and he barely passed two major tests. He was just about to say, "I don't know," when it hit him. "Did the letter from the East Coast Dance Contest come, are we going or not?"

Jennifer said, "start packing your bags, we have a week until the big day! We are going by bus next Friday after school and the contest starts on Saturday in the morning. I'm going to call Mrs. Lands and find out what her plan is for us now."

The week went by so quickly. Alex and Jennifer still could not believe they were actually accepted.

As Jennifer, Alex and their parents waited for the bus, Alex had read the letter over and over. The only thought he had was that he was going to make sure that they came home with the first place trophy. But then he started to feel a little nervous. What if he did something wrong and it caused them not to get first place?

"Jennifer," he asked, "would you be upset if we didn't win? Are we really sure we want to go through with this?"

Jennifer couldn't believe what she was hearing. "Alex, why are you being so negative? You were the one who assured me that this was the right thing to do. We have been practicing all this time, we can't back out now."

Alex thought about all the hard work they had put toward their dancing in the last couple years. For some reason it seemed so different now. He couldn't even picture the dance steps in his mind.

The two hour bus ride seemed to take forever. Mrs. Lands was at the bus station in New York to greet them. She had arrived earlier that day so she could set everything up for them when they arrived. She took one look at Alex and she knew he was suffering from cold feet. Mrs. Lands said, "The dance studio is only a block away, so we are all going to get something good to eat and then we have to get right down to practicing our routine. I have some really good ideas to work on and I already know who the other contestants are, so we have got to get to work right away." Alex and Jennifer's parents went to their hotel to check in and get some rest while Alex and Jennifer were doing their dance practice.

After dinner, Alex felt better and as he got dressed to practice, something came over him, as if he had never had any doubts at all. He thought for a minute, looked at himself in the mirror of the dressing room and said to himself, "I refuse to let Jennifer down, she's worked so hard so we could enter this contest."

Practice was perfect. Jennifer said, "Alex you were perfect and wonderful, you just danced better than you've ever danced."

Mrs. Lands agreed, "All we need now is a good night's sleep and we will meet tomorrow morning at 10:00 am sharp in the dressing room." They said, "Good night" to each other, and they went right to their rooms above the dance studio they would be performing at in the morning. Not a word was said as he looked at her. They exchanged winks. They both knew they were 100% ready for tomorrow. Mrs. Lands was knocking on each of their doors at 9:00 am. "Okay, we better eat a light breakfast, we will have juice and toast or a muffin when we go down to the cafe." Jennifer was starving, but she knew eating the wrong food would be harmful for the competition. Alex didn't seem to mind, he rarely ate breakfast. By 9:45 am they were finished eating and on their way to the dressing room. When they got to the dressing room, Alex and Jennifer's parents were there waiting to greet them both and give them a hug. Alex said, "Thank you so much. I will do my very best for us to win this contest." Their parents gave them a thumbs up and went out to sit in the audience area to watch the competition.

 

It wasn't until then, that Jennifer turned to Alex and said, "If you feel that you have to do this for me, please let me know. I would never forgive myself if you went through all this only to please me, Alex."

Alex turned and softly kissed her on the forehead. "No, dear Jennifer, I am doing this because I love to dance and we both are a team, a team that can't be beat!"

As each team completed their dance, scores were put up on a monitor so everyone could see how the judges scored them. The highest score for the competition was a 10. There were four scores possible. The first one was being judged on the outfits they wore, the second and third scores were for the ability of timing and rhythm of the music, and the fourth one was based on any mistakes made during their dance. Alex and Jennifer saw many different scores shown on the monitor while they were waiting for their turn to go out on the dance floor. After several of the other teams of competition completed, it was about 11:30 am when the competition announcer called, "Miss Jennifer Rice and Mr. Alex Link please come out onto the dance floor."

Jennifer was wearing her bright pink outfit and Alex had on his black tux with a bright pink collar and bright pink stripes down the sides of his pants. The colors made them light up the dance floor. They only heard the announcer as they were gracefully walking across the floor, arm-in-arm to take their place to begin. They looked directly into each other's eyes and listened for the music to start that was selected for them to dance to. Fortunately the music was perfect for the dance routine they had been practicing for.

Alex could feel the strength and power from Jennifer as they danced from one corner to the other across the dance floor. Jennifer felt all the same strength and power from Alex, only this time it was stronger than ever. He picked her up and twirled her above his head. She came down ever so smoothly. The timing to the music was perfect. Alex heard the audience applause and this made him feel unstoppable. He lifted Jennifer two more times, and she met the floor two more times as smoothly as the first, still in time with the music.

As the music came to an end Alex lifted Jennifer above his head and then down for a swoop between his legs and then back up onto her feet for their final break. They faced the audience and bowed just as the music stopped. Nothing could have been more perfect.

As they looked up at the monitor the numbers told the score. 10 - 10 - 10 - and finally, another 10.

Mrs. Lands ran out on the dance floor and gave them both a hug. She shouted, "You did it, You did it!!" They walked back to the waiting area to hear the final points of the other contestants. Alex started biting his nails as he was so nervous. Jennifer said, "Alex, please stop biting your nails, even if we don't win, we need to be happy because at least we got the chance of a life time being accepted to this wonderful contest."

In the next five minutes the winners were announced. The announcer called the winners to come out onto the dance floor. He called the third place winners, the second place winners and then over all of the applause, whistles and names being shown on the main screen, the announcer said, "Our first place winners are, Miss Jennifer Rice and Mr. Alex Link,

Congratulations to all of our winning contestants." All the winners were shaking hands and giving hugs to one another. The dance floor was crowded with so many people.

Alex felt like he was dreaming. He was speechless. Finally after a few minutes he said, "I'm in shock, Jennifer. It all seems like a dream. We really did it!"

Jennifer said, "I knew you had it when you were lifting me up Alex. They weren't able to keep the applause away from us. The music was all I could hear. It's going to take a long time for my heart to stop racing. Our dreams have come true. Thank You Alex, you're the best."

Alex said, "No Jennifer, you are the best." Mrs. Lands walked over to them and gave them a big hug. While they were standing together in amazement, Alex and

Jennifer's parents walked onto the dance floor with a big bouquet of flowers for both Alex and Jennifer. They also gave both Alex and Jennifer hugs.

Jennifer turned to look behind her and noticed two men standing by the railing looking at her. She walked over to Mrs. Lands and asked, "Who are those men standing there?" Mrs. Lands said, "I didn't want to tell you before the competition, but we had some college scouts here today to observe all the dancers. I felt if you knew they were here at the time of your competition, you may have gotten nervous and failed to do the best performance. These gentlemen are from the colleges you and Alex have applied to go to after you graduate high school."

Jennifer walked back over to Alex as he was standing with his parents and asked him if he knew anything about these so called "College Scouts?" He told her he had no idea that they were there and why. Jennifer told him what Mrs. Lands told her about why they were there. Alex asked Jennifer, "so does that mean we are going to be accepted to the colleges we applied for?" Jennifer said, "Let's go ask Mrs. Lands and find out."

As they walked through the crowd of people, they heard Mrs. Lands talking to Jennifer's parents about the college acceptance plans that were in process. Jennifer and Alex walked up to her and interrupted their conversation. Alex asked Mrs. Lands, "What are we supposed to do if these men come over here and start asking us questions?" Mrs. Lands told Alex and Jennifer, "This is a decision you will make with your parents, I'm sure you will be getting a notice in the mail about your performance today and also what college will most likely be the one that will accept you." Alex was thinking about the colleges he applied to. One



The Big Dance

of them was right in New York where they had their competition and the other one was in Florida. He was hoping that the Florida college was who accepted him. He asked Jennifer, "What colleges did you apply to?" Jennifer said, "I applied to a community college in New Jersey and another one here in New York. I guess we'll have to wait and see what college we get accepted to based on our winning the East Coast Dance Competition. We might be going to the same college together Alex." Alex said, "I'm sorry Jennifer, but I applied to a college in Florida and I'm hoping that I get accepted to that one." Jennifer actually was more interested in going to the college she applied for here in New York. Mainly because it was a better college for dance classes she wanted to study for.

While they were talking about colleges, Alex and Jennifer's parents suggested that they get their bags packed and go have lunch. After that they were going to get ready to head back home on the bus and talk more about their plans for college. Mrs. Lands said, "I will join you for lunch and then I have to meet with some of the officials from the competition to go over more information about our school and my dance class instruction position with the school." As they all met for lunch, Alex said, "I don't know about you guys, but I'm starving." Jennifer said, "I'm hungry too. I guess it's because we had to eat a really small breakfast." Alex and Jennifer's parents placed the lunch order for everyone and when they were all sitting at the table eating, a group of waitress's and waiter's came out of the kitchen area carrying a cake with lit candles and singing, "Congratulations Jennifer and Alex, New York's East Coast Dance Winners." Alex looked at his parents and asked, "Did you tell them about us winning?" His mom said, "Yes, we are so proud of you both that we wanted to celebrate and when we get home we are going to plan a celebration for the rest of the family to come and cheer you both on. We are so proud of you both." The cake was decorated with pink and blue icing and a little statue of two people dancing. Jennifer said, "It's so nice, I feel like I don't want to cut it." Alex said, "Jennifer we have to eat a slice to let everyone know how thankful we are for all their support and love."

Then Mrs. Lands told them that they will be awarded a scholarship from their high school also for winning the dance competition. It will be put towards each of their college tuitions for their freshman year. Alex and Jennifer were so amazed with all the prizes they were getting for being the winners of the East Coast Dance Contest. Jennifer said, "Mrs. Lands, I want to continue dancing while I'm in college, but I really want to be a dance instructor like you. I know for a fact that Alex and I would never have gotten the chance to be in the East Coast Dance Contest if it weren't for you. You are such a wonderful teacher." Alex put his arm across Mrs. Lands shoulder and said, "She's right, if it weren't for you there's no way we would be here in the winners spot. We will really miss you when we go to college next year." Mrs. Lands told them she will miss them both too. She said, "I have plans for the next group of students that join my dance class. I want to make arrangements for them to meet you both and I would like you to give them the encouragement they need to have, so they will want to enter the next East Coast Dance Contest. I intend to enter my most advanced students each year for this contest. It would be wonderful if others could be first, second or third place winners."

Alex looked at his watch and saw that it was almost time for them to go to the bus station and get their bus home. He was anxious to get home and get some rest after such an eventful and tiring couple of days. "Well, Alex said, It's time for us to head out to the bus station and go home?" Mrs. Lands, Jennifer, her parents and Alex's parents picked up their bags and they all started walking out of the lunch cafe' to get the bus home. Mrs. Lands said, "Thank you for a wonderful lunch" to Jennifer and Alex's parents. She also let them know that she had made arrangements to meet with the gentlemen from the dance contest after they all arrived home. The bus was ready for them to board when they got to the bus station.

After they got settled in their seats, Alex asked his mom, "What is Mrs. Lands going to contact you about?" Alex's mom told him, "Mrs. Lands is making sure that you and Jennifer get trophies and certificates for winning First Place. She is also making sure that the college scouts are given all the information they need to complete the applications for each of the colleges you both applied to." She told him that Jennifer's parents, her and his dad had already taken care of the paperwork they needed to complete.

Alex said, "Mom do you feel comfortable with me going to Florida for college?" His mom said, "Alex, you are the one to decide the college you feel you are most comfortable with to attend for the next four years. Even though it is a longer distance away then New York, the most important thing is that you get the education you need for the classes you want to take."

Alex said, "I'm planning on taking Business classes because I feel that I would like to start a business of my own rather than having to work for someone." His mom was thinking about what she remembered Jennifer talking to Mrs. Land's about earlier. Jennifer mentioned that she wanted to be a dance instructor like Mrs. Lands and that was what she was looking forward to doing in college. She looked at Alex and asked him, "Did you hear Jennifer tell Mrs. Lands that she wanted to be a dance instructor?" "Yes," Alex said.

He got up from his seat on the bus and went back to where Jennifer and her parents were sitting. He looked at Jennifer and said, "Jennifer can I ask you something?" Jennifer said, "Sure Alex." He asked her about her intentions on being a dance instructor like she told Mrs. Lands. He told her that he was going to take business classes in college and he thought that maybe when they completed their classes, maybe he could open a dance class business studio and Jennifer could be the dance instructor like she wanted to be. Jennifer was so impressed with Alex's idea. She said, "Alex, what an awesome idea, we can work together even after we get out of college, actually even if you own the business, you can be an instructor too, since you have all the experience with dancing like I do. Lets do it, we can have Mrs. Lands help us with setting everything up." Alex said, "I'm going back to my seat and think about this until we get home." "Okay," Jennifer said, and she pushed her seat back so she could lay back and get some rest during the rest of the drive home.

As Jennifer was resting, many thoughts went through her mind. Some she felt were not so interesting, but a few she thought were going to be so beneficial to her and Alex. Several times as she was thinking, she looked up toward where Alex was sitting and noticed him starring at her in a strange way. All through the years, she couldn't remember him ever looking or starring at her like that. After about a half hour,



The Big Dance

Jennifer started to feel sleepy and decided to go to sleep for the rest of the ride home.

Jennifer was woken up all of a sudden by sounds of horns and sirens all around the bus. She looked to where Alex was sitting and he wasn't there. She didn't see his parents either. "Oh My," she thought, "What is going on?" She turned to the seats where her parents and Mrs. Lands were sitting and no-one was there! Actually, the more she looked around the bus, she noticed that almost everyone was not on the bus at all.

Jennifer got up out of her seat and walked down the aisle to the front of the bus and she saw many Police cars with their lights flashing and as she tried to get off the bus a Police Officer stopped her and told her she had to stay inside. Jennifer looked back to where everyone was sitting and still did not see them. Several other people were still on the bus and she could hear some crying coming from some of the people still on the bus with her. As she went to see who the people were and try to find out if they knew what happened, she saw Mrs. Lands laying across the floor at the seat she was sitting at. "Mrs. Lands," Jennifer said, in a quiet voice. She got no response from her at all. Jennifer lifted Mrs. Lands arm up and it fell right back down by her side. Jennifer noticed there was blood coming from the side of Mrs. Lands head. She got up and ran to the front of the bus and yelled to the Police Officer, "Help, Please help, my teacher, Mrs. Lands is laying on the floor and she is bleeding from her head. Someone needs to come into the bus right now and help her." The Police Officer opened the bus door and waved for an ambulance worker to come onto the bus with him. Just as the door opened and Jennifer looked outside she could



The Big Dance

see a lot of people laying on the ground and nurses all around them. She said to the Police Officer, "Sir my family and my friend and his family aren't on the bus right now and I don't know where they are. Can I go outside and see if I can find them." He told her she had to wait until he made sure it was safe and the rest of the people on the bus weren't hurt.

As he and the nurse who came on the bus with him to help Mrs. Lands, looked for the others that were still on the bus, they found they weren't injured but were crying because they weren't able to get off the bus either. They told the Police Officer that they didn't know what happened or how their families got off the bus.

Jennifer started walking to the front of the bus before the Police Officer and he grabbed her hand and said, "I will take you off the bus and we will walk through the ambulances so you can see if any of your friends and family are injured and need to be taken to the closest hospitals." At that point, Jennifer started to panic. "Please Officer tell me what happened?" "Okay," he said, "the bus came to a stop light and an outside passenger got on the bus and he had a gun. He made everyone get out of their seats and get off the bus immediately. When they all got off the bus he started to threaten them with his gun to hand over their money and any valuables they had. At that point, most of the people who had valuables gave them to him, but those who didn't have any or wouldn't give them to him is when he began to shoot at them to enforce them to do what he said. Some of the people got hurt badly and are in the ambulances now getting treated for their injuries. Other people are laying on the ground so they wouldn't get shot.



The Big Dance

The Police Officer and the nurse from the ambulance were able to wake Mrs. Lands up and help her to sit in her seat on the bus. Jennifer went and sat next to her while the nurse examined her head injury. Mrs. Lands said, "Jennifer where is everyone and what is going on?" Jennifer told Mrs. Lands, "We need to make sure you are okay so don't worry about what happened right now." The nurse was taking care of Mrs. Lands and said, "You must have fallen and hit the side of your head on the metal bar under the seat across from where you were sitting. You may need a few stitches and I will take care of that for you." She also asked Mrs. Lands, "Do you have a headache or do you feel dizzy?" Mrs. Lands said, "Not really, I only feel confused since I have no idea what is happening and how did I get hurt? Also, where are all the other passengers on the bus, my students Alex, his parents and Jennifer's parents are not here."

The Police Officer explained the situation to Mrs. Lands and then Jennifer asked the nurse, "Can Mrs. Lands come with me after you take care of her head so we can go look for Alex, his parents and my parents?" The nurse said, "Yes, but I will have to stay with you both just incase Mrs. Lands does start to feel a little dizzy." It took about fifteen minutes and the nurse had Mrs. Lands all taken care of so they started to walk off the bus to find Alex, his parents and Jennifer's parents. The Police Officer went with them also. As they were walking, another Police Officer came to them and mentioned that everything was taken care of with the man that had the gun. They took him to the local jail. He told them they were safe as they were walking around.

Mrs. Lands did not feel dizzy as they were walking toward the ambulances and Jennifer was so relieved. She was still worried about everyone else. They got to the first ambulance and didn't see anyone inside. As they were walking toward the next ambulance, Mrs. Lands heard someone yelling, "Over here, we are over here." Both Jennifer and Mrs. Lands looked at each other in surprise and when they looked toward where they heard the yelling come from, it was Alex. Jennifer ran over to him and everyone else was with him laying behind a big table. Mrs. Lands and the nurse got there a few minutes later and the nurse made sure no-one was in need of any medical help. Jennifer's mom told the nurse that when the man with the gun made them get off the bus, they gave him their money and when he turned around to grab other people, they saw the big table and they ran over to it and hid behind it so the man wouldn't come after them again. Mrs. Lands and Jennifer walked behind the table and sat down with Alex, his parents and her parents and just put their arms around each other.

The Police Officer let them know they didn't have to stay behind the table now and he would walk them back to the bus so they can get ready to continue their way home. The bus driver was not injured and almost everyone that was on the bus seemed to be okay. There were only a few people that had to go to the hospital because they got hurt really bad. As everyone was going back to get on the bus, Alex put his arm around Jennifer's shoulder and told her he was so glad that they all were ok. He asked her what happened to Mrs. Lands. Jennifer told him that she must have gotten up to get off the bus and somehow she fell and hit her head on a metal bar on the seat across from the seat she was sitting in. She was unconscious for awhile too. The nurse took care of her head and had to put about three stitches there. She told him that Mrs. Lands was feeling ok and should be able to go right back to work at the dance studio.

When they got to the bus, Jennifer's mom and dad gave everyone a hug and said they were so thankful that everyone was ok. They all got back to the seats they were sitting in and the bus driver announced that he was ready to continue the ride back. He told them they were about a half hour away from the bus station. If anyone needs to call for a ride they could make their call now. Fortunately, Mrs. Lands, Jennifer, Alex and their parents had parked their cars at the bus station so they could go right home.

While they were on the bus ride home, Jennifer went to sit next to Alex. She said, "I am really glad we had such a wonderful experience winning the Dance Contest, but it just seems so strange that this happened to us, a crazy man with a gun got on the bus when it was stopped at a red light and created all this scary stuff." Alex said, "Jennifer I feel the same way, when I was hiding behind the table with our parents, I realized you and Mrs. Lands weren't with us and I was so worried about you both. I ran off the bus with our parents and I thought you and Mrs. Lands were with us.

The man had us up against the side of the bus with lots of other people that were on the bus too, and he started making everyone hand over their money and any jewelry that they had. Everyone gave him something and when he had it all in a bag he was holding, he turned around to look for more people and our parents saw a table by the back of the bus and we all ran over to it and hid behind it. That's when we realized you and Mrs. Lands weren't with us. Our parents and I were so worried about where

                            The Big Dance

you and Mrs. Lands were and thought that the man might have hurt both of you. We could see inside the bus from behind the table and I thought I saw you and a Police Officer walking inside the bus. I told your mom and dad what I saw and they both kept watching and realized it was you. But we still didn't know where Mrs. Lands was. After that, I remembered that before all this happened I saw you sleeping. So I guess you slept through everything when the man was making people get off the bus. He might have only made anyone he saw that he thought had money or valuables get off the bus and since he saw you sleeping and you didn't have anything valuable next to you or on your lap, he just went to the next person. Now I know why you ended up being on the bus while all the crazy stuff was going on outside. One of the people on the bus who didn't get off must have called 911 and got the Police to come. If I remember right, I'm thinking it was maybe about fifteen minutes when I saw the Police cars and ambulances pull up and started looking for the man that had the gun. I actually couldn't see him, but I heard lots of people screaming and crying and I started to worry that maybe Mrs. Lands was one of them. I saw some people that tried to run from him and that's when I heard some gun shots. Your parents and my parents were laying behind that table and could hear pretty much everything that was happening. Then I saw you, a nurse, Mrs. Lands and a Police Officer walking off the bus, so I yelled to you all, hoping you would hear me and you did. I was so glad to see that Mrs. Lands was with you, but I saw a bandage on her head and really started to worry what happened to her. Well, lets just try to not concentrate on this and start to think about how much fun we had at the Dance Contest. I know we

 The Big Dance

will never forget this incident, but its better to try and think about how much fun we had this weekend and how important it is for us to stay committed to finishing college and getting started with our plans for our own dance studio." Jennifer agreed with Alex and then asked him if he thought they should go to where Mrs. Lands was sitting on the bus and check on how she was doing. Alex said, "Yes, lets go see if she is okay."

While they were walking in the aisle on the bus, the bus driver announced that they would be arriving at the bus station in approximately fifteen minutes. They got to the seat Mrs. Lands was sitting in and noticed she was sleeping. Alex's mom said, "Alex, Mrs. Lands is okay, she has been resting since we all got back on the bus." Jennifer looked at Alex and said, "I hope she is going to be able to come back to the dance studio on Monday, when we have our next dance lessons." Alex said, "You know what Jennifer, if Mrs. Lands isn't able to then I will help out and take care of her plans for the lessons she has scheduled. It would be better for her to rest for the next couple of days." Jennifer agreed with Alex. "Actually," she said, "we both could make sure all the lessons for the rest of the week get done for her, because this is our last week of school before graduation. We need to work on a plan for our graduation dance too." Alex said, "Oh my Jennifer, you're right. Maybe we should perform the same dance that we did at the dance contest. Our senior classmates will be so proud of us and it would be great for us to let them see the dance we did to win first place." Jennifer said, "Alex, that is such a good idea, I know Mrs. Lands would really want us to do that too."

The bus pulled into the bus station and Alex gently tapped Mrs. Lands on her shoulder to wake her up and let her know. Mrs. Lands slowly opened her eyes and looked at Alex. She said, "Are we at the bus station?" Alex nodded yes and told her he would carry her things and help her to her car. Mrs. Lands asked him if she could get a ride home with him and his parents because she didn't feel like she was able to drive her car.

Alex turned around to where his parents were sitting and let them know that Mrs. Lands needed a ride from the bus station to her house. His dad said, "I will drive Mrs. Lands home in our car and your mom and Jennifer can drive Mrs. Lands car to her house so she doesn't have to leave it at the bus station. Then we can make sure she is okay before we leave to go home." Alex went back to Mrs. Lands and told her the plan and she was very pleased.

Jennifer and her parents were all together and Alex went to their seats and told them the plan they had to make sure Mrs. Lands got home okay. Jennifer said, "Oh Alex, I hope she is going to be okay. We need to tell her our plans to schedule the dance classes this week so she can stay home and rest. I'm sure she will be glad we can take care of classes for her." Alex told Jennifer he will explain everything to Mrs. Lands while they are driving her home.

Everyone got off the bus and walked to the parking lot to get in their cars to leave. Mrs. Lands, Jennifer, Alex and their parents all said, "Thank You," to each other and gave hugs. Jennifer told Alex she will see him tomorrow at the dance studio right after school.

"Getting ready for graduation Saturday night, will be the next big thing we have to get ready for," Jennifer said. Alex said, "I'm going to wear the same tux that

I wore at the dance contest, so why don't you wear the same dress you wore too." Jennifer said, "that's a good idea Alex, then I won't have to go shopping to find something else."

When they all got to their cars, everyone said, "Goodnight," and left to go home.

As Alex and his Dad were driving Mrs. Lands home, Alex told Mrs. Lands that Jennifer and him will take care of teaching the dance classes for the rest of the week so she could rest and not have to worry about all the other students missing the classes. Mrs. Lands said, "Alex you and Jennifer are so wonderful, I was concerned about my students, you and Jennifer missing classes all week. I know you and Jennifer will be able to take care of everything for the rest of the week. Thank you so much. Please don't forget you both have to get ready for graduation Saturday night.

I don't know what I would do without you." Alex asked her if she would want to be one of the dance coaches when he and Jennifer completed college and opened up their own dance studio. Mrs. Lands told him that she needed to continue teaching dance classes at the studio she was at, but if they needed her help with anything they could always let her know and she would help with whatever they needed. Alex said, "If for some reason you have to close your dance studio, you can let us know and then be a part of our dance studio. I feel you have so much more experience than us and it would be so helpful to get us started." Mrs. Lands said, "I will help you even if I'm still working at my studio. I'll make sure you both have everything you need. I'm so proud of you for planning to start your own dance studio after you graduate from college. I know it will be at least four years until you both graduate so I will put a packet together so you can start from step one."

Mrs. Lands advised Alex that both him and Jennifer needed to started a bank account and put money away to start their own business. She told him she would go through her paperwork from when she opened her dance studio many years ago and let both him and Jennifer know what it might cost them. She also mentioned that prices would most likely be more now than when she started her studio. She also let Alex know that if they needed any help in getting a loan, she would give them anything they needed. Alex told Mrs. Lands that he was only concentrating on his college tuition and would plan taking care of the cost to start the dance studio during his last year of college. Then Alex's dad said, "Alex, don't forget that you do have some money that you already put in an account to help pay for college, but when you found out that you won the dance contest and it would pay your way through college, you should be able to use it for whatever it might cost to start our own business, and also I'm sure Jennifer's parents will help with both of you planning to start your own business also." Alex said, "Yes dad, you're right, when we get home lets talk to them and see if we can all make plans together."

It was just a few minutes after Mrs. Lands, Alex and his dad were discussing their future plans, that they pulled into the driveway of Mrs. Lands house. Jennifer, her mom and Alex's mom drove in right behind them. Just as they all were getting out of their cars, a big party van drove into the driveway also, and as the van doors opened all the senior student classmates jumped out with balloons and decorations yelling, "Congratulations!!!" How exciting it was to be back home again for both Alex and Jennifer. Even

Mrs. Lands didn't know the senior classmates were going to surprise them. After the classmates all got to congratulate Jennifer, Alex, and Mrs. Lands, they said, "We'll see you in school on Monday, everyone is so proud of you." Then they all got back into the party van and left.

Before everyone went home to quiet down and rest, Mrs. Lands, Alex and his dad explained to Jennifer, her mom and dad, the plans that they talked about as they were driving home. Everyone agreed that this would be the best way to work everything out. Now all they had to do was plan for graduation at the end of the week which would be another exciting part of their week. Then they would have the entire Summer to plan for starting college. Alex did tell Jennifer that they needed to keep in touch with each other while they were away during their college years. After all, they were best friends and knew that they could be the professional dance partners in their own business together one day. Jennifer and Alex's mom and dad were so excited and thankful for all the work Mrs. Lands put into teaching their children all about dance and now their lives in the future after college would be all set for being able to continue on just like Mrs. Lands.

The End